D0966471

SUPER RABBIT BOY VS. SUPER RABBIT BOSS!

READ MORE

PRESS START!

BOOKS!

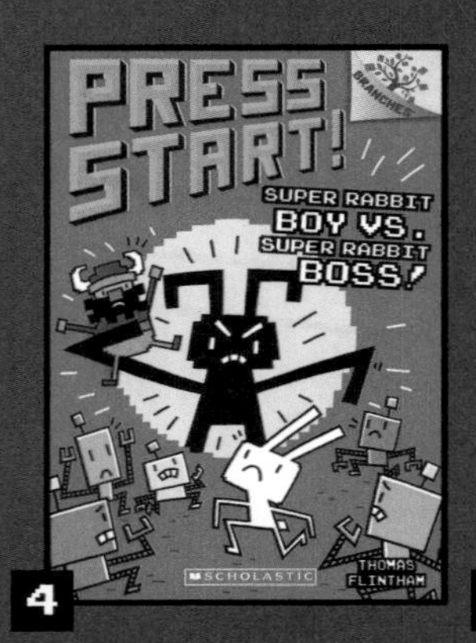

MORE BOOKS COMING SOON

THOMAS FLINTHAM

BRANCHES™
SCHOLASTIC INC.

FOR BELLA AND TED

Library of Congress Cataloging-in-Publication Data

Names: Flintham, Thomas, author, illustrator.
Title: Super Rabbit Boy vs. Super Rabbit Boss! / by Thomas Flintham.
Other titles: Super Rabbit Boy versus Super Rabbit Boss
Description: First edition. | New York : Branches/Scholastic Inc., 2018. |
Series: Press start! | Summary: Super Rabbit Boy falls down a pipe and discovers himself in a mirror reality where everyone good is now evil, including his mirror self, Super Rabbit Boss, and he must make friends with King Viking (now one of the good guys) and somehow defeat his alter ego in order to save this world—and somehow find a way back to his own reality.
Identifiers: LCCN 2017033592| ISBN 9781338034752 (pbk.) | ISBN 9781338034769 (bound library edition)
Subjects: LCSH: Superheroes—Juvenile fiction. | Supervillains—Juvenile fiction. | Animals—Juvenile fiction. | Identity (Psychology)—Juvenile fiction. | Video games—Juvenile fiction. | CYAC: Superheroes—Fiction. | Supervillains—Fiction. | Animals—Fiction. | Identity—Fiction. | Video games—Fiction.
Classification: LCC PZ7.1.F585 Sv 2017 | DDC [Fic]—dc23 LC record available at https://lccn.loc.gov/2017033

15 14 13 20 21 22 23 24

Printed in the U.S.A. 40
First edition, February 2018
Edited by Celia Lee
Book design by Maria Mercado

TABLE OF CONTENTS

1 PRESS START!

This is Animal Town. It is a happy place. But meanie King Viking likes to attack the town with his Robot Army.

He is causing even more trouble this time. He has kidnapped Singing Dog again. Plus, he has taken Simon the Hedgehog and Celia Crocodile, too! They're trapped in Boom Boom Factory, King Viking's home.

Don't worry! Super Rabbit Boy is here. He will save the day.

He sets out for Boom Boom Factory.

To get to Boom Boom Factory, Super Rabbit Boy must get through three levels. First, Super Rabbit Boy chases King Viking's robots out of Lovely Woods.

Then he swims across the Sunny Sea.

Next, the Creepy Caves are full of mazes!
ıey don't slow Super Rabbit Boy down. He
ıns faster than ever. And he jumps on all
e robots in his way.

At last, he leaves the caves. He's right in front of Boom Boom Factory.

Super Rabbit Boy searches Boom Boom Factory for his friends.

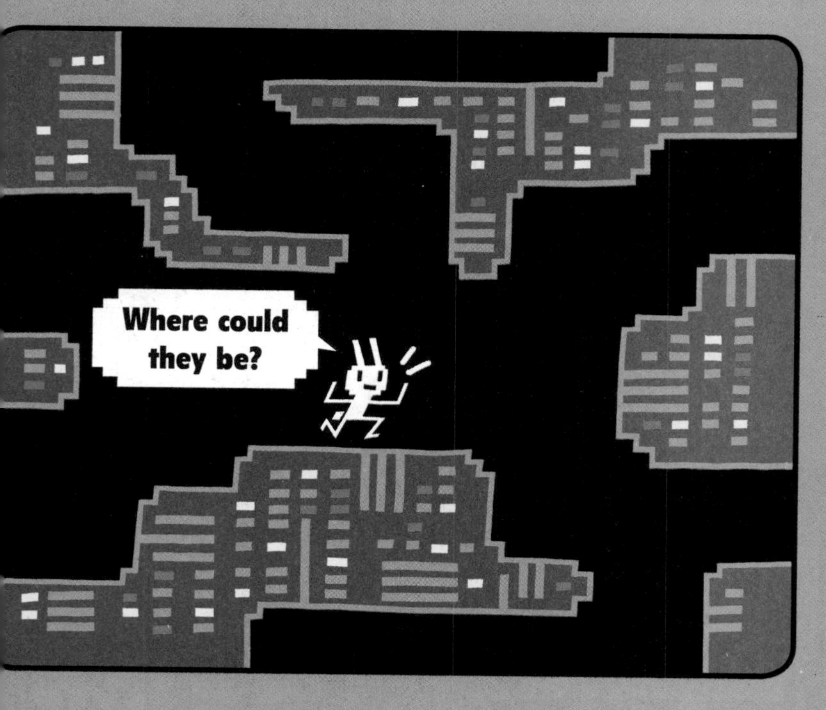

Super Rabbit Boy steps into a room full of bolts, wrenches, and all sorts of metal parts.

This must be King Viking's workshop! It's where he builds his creations.

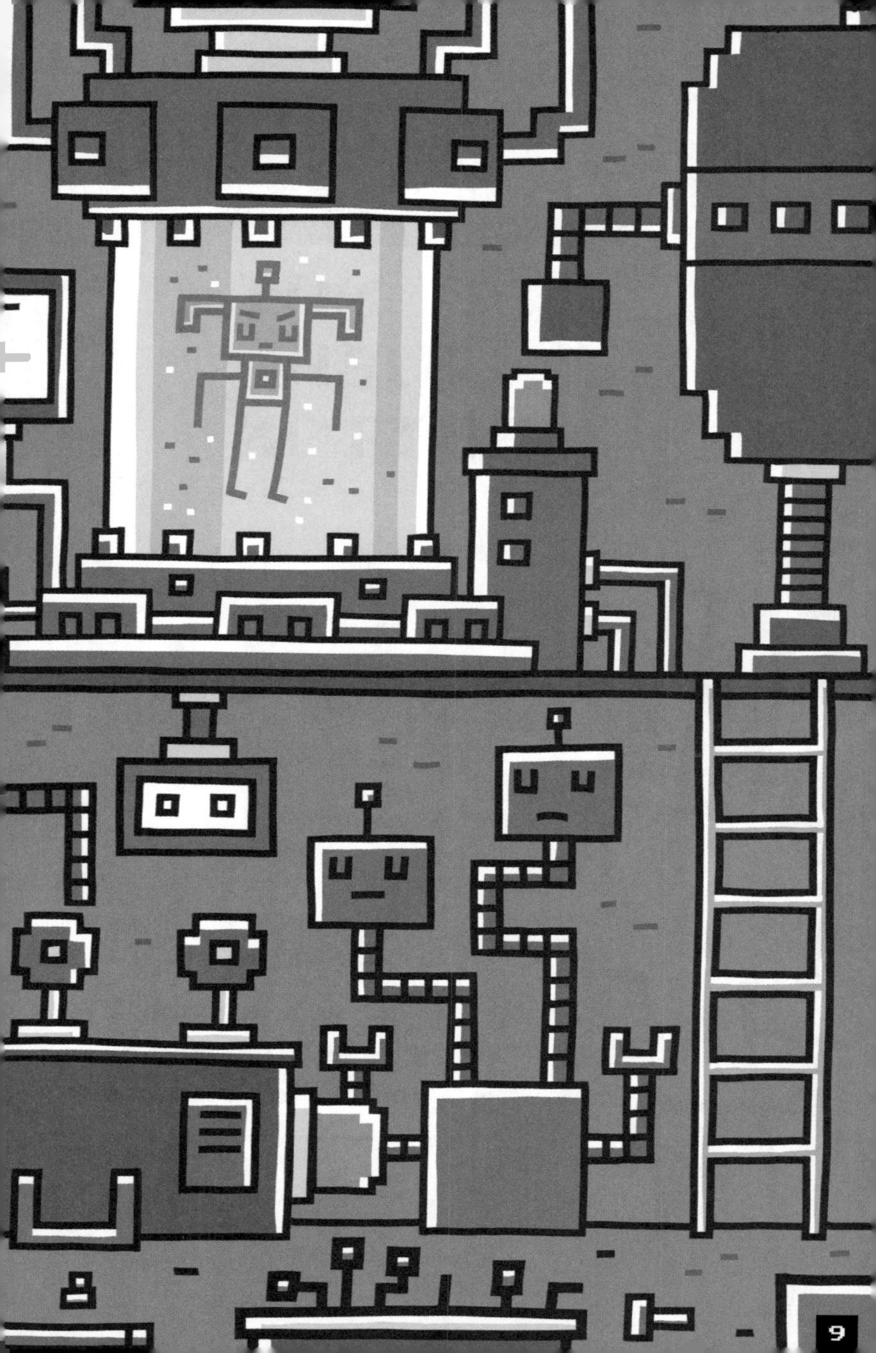

Super Rabbit Boy spots a strange machin in the corner. There is a large warning sign next to it.

DO NOT PUSH BUTTON
Do not push that button? Ha! It's a trick. This must be an entrance to a secret room!

Boing! Boing!
Here I . . .

Gooooooooooooo!
BEEP!
BOING!

Yikes! Super Rabbit Boy is in trouble!

2 THE SAME BUT DIFFERENT

After falling for a long, long time, Supe
Rabbit Boy sees a light.
At last! A way out.
BOING!

TFX
Waaahh! Am I back? This looks like the room I was in before. But something is different.

Suddenly, a robot walks into the room. H
sees Super Rabbit Boy and shouts!

More robots run into the room. They all start crying when they see Super Rabbit Boy!

Super Rabbit Boy is surprised.

The robots are confused. Then one steps
rward.

One of the blue robots smiles and turns to the other robots.

Aha! We're safe! This must be Super Rabbit Boss's mirror twin from the Mirror World!

3 THE MIRROR WORLDS

per Rabbit Boy is very confused.

What is a mirror twin? Where is the Mirror World?
We will tell you everything.

There are two worlds. Your world and our world.
The two worlds are mirror images of each other. They are almost the same, but there are some big differences.

Everything good in your world is bad in our world.
Everything bad in your world is good in our world.

We have the big, bad, meanie Super Rabbit Boss in our world. But you are his Mirror World twin. So you must be really nice.
I try to be nice all the time. Wait a minute! Does that mean your King Viking is nice?
Yes! We call him Good King Viking. He is super nice!

Well, my King Viking is SUPER MEAN all the time! His robots are mean, too!
We are not mean!
We were built to be nice!

All the robots burst into tears again!

The robots explain that Super Rabbit Boss
ants their whole world to be mean and
orrible. Good King Viking always does nice
ings, so Super Rabbit Boss captured him.
e is a prisoner in Carrot Castle.

Don't worry. I can save your king!
We will come, too!
Maybe we can help!
Okay! Boing! Boing! Let's go rescue Good King Viking!

4 INTO THE CRYSTAL CAVES

o get to Carrot Castle, Super Rabbit Boy ust get through three levels. First, Super abbit Boy and the robots head toward the rystal Caves.

The Crystal Caves are much nicer than the Creepy Caves in Super Rabbit Boy's world.

These caves are so pretty! In my world, they are dark and scary!
We love these caves!
The crystals make great presents!

The Crystal Caves are pretty, but they are
till full of mazes.

Super Rabbit Boy follows the robots all
e way through the caves to the exit.

It's Simon the Horrible Hedgehog!
You will have to get past me first!
Oh boop!

5 FAST PROBLEMS

The robots burst into tears. Simon the Horrible Hedgehog runs in circles around the group. He's very fast! How will they stop him?

The robots are busy crying. But Super Rabbit Boy is busy thinking.

We need to find a way to stop Simon. I am just as fast as he is. But he's too spiky for me to grab.
We could use our metal hands to grab him. But he is too quick.
That's it! You might not be as fast as he is, but there are more of you!

Super Rabbit Boy makes all the robots ·and in a circle. They extend their arms in ·ont of them.

The robots grab at the same time. One of the robots catches Simon the Horrible Hedgehog!

Super Rabbit Boy and the robots tie up
imon the Horrible Hedgehog. They head
ut the exit.

6 CHOMPY SEAS

The Stormy Sea lies ahead of the group. It looks very gloomy.

The Sunny Sea in my world is much nicer! Can you robots swim?
We can! Good King Viking made us out of very rare waterproof parts.

We're his only waterproof things.
That's why we can cry.
You do cry a lot.
Good King Viking says it's good to show our feelings. So when we feel scared or sad, we cry.
WELL, YOU BETTER START CRYING!

A big, scary crocodile bursts from the sea
The robots start to cry.

How will Super Rabbit Boy and the robots feat Celia the Crunching Crocodile?

Super Rabbit Boy has an idea!

The robots start building. They're very
st!

The crystal boat is ready. It looks really strong. But is it strong enough to beat Celi and her crunching crocodile teeth?

The boat sails into the Stormy Sea. Celia
not happy.

Celia swims straight toward the crystal
ɔat!

Celia swoops in and bites the side of th
boat.

7 NOISE IN THE WOODS

per Rabbit Boy checks the side of the
oat. Is it okay?

Oh bloop! I hope the boat is strong enough!

The boat is fine! But Celia's crunching crocodile teeth are not. They are broken!

Hooray!
We're safe!
Waaaaa!

It is Celia's turn to cry!

The crystal boat sails smoothly past the
ying crocodile.

The sea is stormy, but the crystal boat is strong and fast. Soon they see land!

Super Rabbit Boy and the robots jump
to the shore.

They are close to Carrot Castle. But the
eird Woods stand in their way. They are
t like the Lovely Woods. They look spooky!
e robots start to cry.

The robots are scared, but they follow Super Rabbit Boy into the woods. They are still crying.

Suddenly, a loud noise shakes the whole woods!

The robots cry even more!
BEEP! BOOP!
BOOP! BEEP!
What was that?
IT WAS ME —

<u>Shouting</u> Dog!

WOOOOOOOOOOF.

8 WOOF VS. BEEP!

houting Dog lets out a super loud bark. he bark is so powerful that it blows Super abbit Boy and the robots back to the hore.

His voice doesn't sound as nice as Singing Dog!
Oh boop!
What a scary sound!

Super Rabbit Boy starts thinking of a plan

Super Rabbit Boy and the robots know hat to do! They get right to work. They alk back into the woods. Shouting Dog nds them, but they are ready.

Shouting Dog starts barking, but the robots are not scared. They've built a giant megaphone with the boat's crystals! They all shout into it!

Keep going, robots! You can do it!

BOOOOOOOOOP!

WOOOOOOOOOF!

Shouting Dog is loud, but the robots are louder! They blast him backward.

He is blasted far, far away.

Look out, Super Rabbit Boss! Super Rabbit Boy and the robots are on the way!

9 BATTLE OF THE RABBITS

Super Rabbit Boy and the robots arrive at Carrot Castle.

Boing! Boing! Here we are!
Oh beep!
Oh boop!

This Carrot Castle is much creepier than the Carrot Castle in Super Rabbit Boy's world.

Don't worry. I'll deal with Super Rabbit Boss. Let's go inside.

Boing! Boing!
Here I am, Super Rabbit Boss!

Super Rabbit Boy and Super Rabbit Boss meet at last!
Bing! Bing! Here I am! You must be the boring mirror of me!

The robots spot Good King Viking in a age. Super Rabbit Boss springs into action! hat is his plan?

Super Rabbit Boss puts on a giant Robo-Rabbit Robot Suit!

The robots start to cry.

Super Rabbit Boss grabs Super Rabbit Boy.

The robots start to cry even more! Is this ame over for Super Rabbit Boy?

10 A TEARFUL ENDING

The robots keep crying and crying. Soon, the room starts to fill with their tears. Suddenly, Super Rabbit Boy remembers something.

Hey, robots! You really are terrible!
He is right!
We are rotten robots!

The robots cry harder. Super Rabbit Boss dances and splashes around with joy.

The Robo-Rabbit Robot Suit starts to shak
and spark.

The robo-suit explodes!

The blast sends Super Rabbit Boss flying
rough the roof of Carrot Castle.

Good King Viking is free!

Super Rabbit Boy gets ready to go back to his world. Good King Viking gives him a present.

This should help you handle your King Viking!

Good-bye! And remember: When you work together, you always win!

We will!

Bye boop!

Bye beep!